By Dave Kilgore:

204 Short Monologues and Scenes for Kids and Teens

Flash Fiction Light, Dark, and Odd-
   150 One-Page Stories of Murder, Grief, Levity, and Love

Murder in Breakbroke Pass-
   A Satirical Southern Novel

100 Short and Effective Monologues

100 More Short and Effective Monologues

Another 100 Short and Effective Monologues

Bite-Size Flash Fiction-
   100 One-Page, Monologue-Style Musings

Flash Fiction in a Flash-
   100 One-Page, Monologue-Style Stories

One-Minute Flash Fiction-
   100 One-Page, Monologue-Style Miniatures

Flash Fiction in a Flash

100 One-Page, Monologue-Style
Stories to Read on the Run

by Dave Kilgore

Flash Fiction in a Flash

Copyright © 2019 by Dave Kilgore.
All rights reserved. No part of this book may be reproduced in any form without written permission from the publisher. For permission requests, contact the publisher through www.scribernautpress.com or on Facebook.

This book is a work of fiction. Any references to historical events; to real people, living or dead; or to real locales are intended only to give the fiction a sense of reality and authenticity. Names, characters, places, and incidents are either the product of the author's imagination or are used fictitiously, and their resemblance, if any, to real-life counterparts is entirely coincidental.
All images in this book have been printed with permission for commercial use and with no attribution required.
Internal Control Number: FFIAF072319B

A Scribernaut Press, LLC Publication
www.scribernautpress.com

This book is dedicated to all the lovers of fictional works of extreme brevity, flash fiction, the momentary encounter, the personal, one-minute blurb from the life of a character, as spoken by that character.

Flash Fiction in a Flash
by Dave Kilgore

This is a book of one-page, monologue-style, flash fiction pieces. All one hundred of them are taken directly from my book, *100 More Short and Effective Monologues: Original, one-minute pieces for adult actors to use in auditions, classroom, and practice.* After writing that book of monologues for my fellow actors, and seeing that the format closely resembled so many of the flash fiction stories I'd previously written, I thought it would be a shame to not share them with all the non-actors who appreciate this style of writing. So, here they are. In this book, I have given you just the flash, minus the interruption by many pages of boring acting tips. Enjoy.

CONTENTS

CONVERSATION STARTER	1
KILLING BARRY	2
ENEMIES FOREIGN AND DOMESTIC	3
FIRST DATES	4
AGORAPHOBIA	5
ON CANVAS	6
VOICES	7
FIRST BIKE	8
SEEDS OF DOUBT	9
PATIENCE	10
FLOWERS FOR BUNNIES	11
HERE'S A TISSUE	12
JUSTICE	13
STAR ATHLETE	14
PLAYING CHECKERS	15
TAKING IT WELL	16
DISAPPROVAL	17
BROWN BAGGING IT	18
COUNT ON YOU	19
TRUCE	20
EXPECTATIONS	21
ALL ON MY OWN	22
REAL MONSTERS	23
WORLD PEACE	24
HIDING PROBLEMS	25
BUBBLE GUM	26
ADDICTION	27
BEING RESPONSIBLE	28
MIND CONTROL	29
LIVE LONG AND PROSPER	30
BRAVE FOOL	31
WAITING IN LINE	32

NO REGRETS	33
HUMORLESS	34
FORCED RETIREMENT	35
NO SECOND PLACE	36
THANKFUL	37
EMPTY CANS	38
I TOLD YOU	39
MASKS	40
DEER IN THE HEADLIGHTS	41
NOT GOING TO GRIEVE	42
INTOLERANT	43
SEEN A GHOST	44
FINE PRINT	45
NOTHING I CAN DO ABOUT IT	46
REPEAT OFFENDER	47
SPACE AND TIME	48
MODERN FORENSICS	49
FORGIVENESS	50
FAVORITES	51
GRATITUDE	52
GUSTO	53
HARD DECISIONS	54
NOT LIKE THAT	55
VOLUNTEER	56
STRAWBERRIES AND HUGS	57
COWARDS	58
KILLING IS EASY	59
LESSONS IN LOVE LOST	60
PROPAGANDA	61
BIRTHDAY SURPRISE	62
BIG BAD MEN	63
CHRISTMAS AT THE MALL	64
DEVIL IN THE DETAILS	65
NEWSPAPERS	66

UNSUBSTANTIATED RAINBOWS	67
FOR A SONG	68
COMPETENCE	69
WORKING TOWARD PEACE	70
FREEDOM	71
BESTSELLING AUTHOR	72
REFUSING GOODBYE	73
SAYING THE WORDS	74
HUNGRY EYES	75
PERFECT LIKENESS	76
FAITH	77
INTENTIONS	78
VICTIM	79
SENTIMENTAL	80
NEED TO KNOW	81
TOGETHER	82
IT'S ALL A GAMBLE	83
SAFE DEPOSIT BOX	84
MISSION CRITICAL	85
MISTAKES	86
FORCE OF NATURE	87
EVEN-TEMPERED	88
CASTING THE ROLE	89
DANGEROUS MISSION	90
TAKING CREDIT	91
STRICTLY BUSINESS	92
DOING THE RIGHT THING	93
WHATEVER YOU WANT	94
WINNING AND LOSING	95
ROAD TRIP	96
INSANE YOUTH	97
BEAUTIFUL NOW	98
OLD TOYS	99
SMILES, EVERYONE	100

"Brevity is."

—*Dave Kilgore*

FLASH FICTION
in a FLASH

CONVERSATION STARTER

I bring a different book to the coffee shop every day. I don't read that much; I hardly read at all, actually. The books are just props. Interesting titles, colorful covers, whatever I think will catch somebody's attention. It's a hobby of mine. I leave the book on the table while I look out the window, sipping my latte, like I'm pondering life or death or the last passage of what I'm insinuating I've just read. *To Kill a Mockingbird. 1984. The Catcher in the Rye.* Different books elicit different responses. Sometimes I'll hear, "Oh, you're reading that? What do you think of it so far?" And I'll say, "Oh, have a seat. I'd love to hear *your* view on it." People love to give their opinions. And I don't really have to know the book to participate. I sip my coffee, I nod, and I give the occasional, "Um hmm," and, "Ah." At the end of the conversation, either I've made a new friend, or I've gotten the condensed version of the book in audio commentary, or both. I'm thinking of taking a copy of *The Joy of Sex* to the coffee shop tomorrow. We'll see how that plays out.

KILLING BARRY

There was just one thing I wanted to do before I died: kill Barry. Ever since high school when he took Janet from me I wanted him dead. I imagined so many scenarios in my mind. Pushing him off the water tower. Drowning him in his own pool. Dropping a piano on his head. Okay, that one was a little cartoony, but hey, they were my fantasies. I started reading murder mysteries, hoping to discover a plan for the perfect crime, where at the end he'd be six feet under and I wouldn't even be considered as a suspect. But the stories always resolved with the culprit going to prison for the rest of his life. I wasn't willing to trade my freedom for revenge. Then I found out last year that Barry dropped dead from a heart attack while playing racquetball. While I wasn't that upset about it, I wasn't thrilled either. I wanted him gone, but I wanted to be the one who took him down. Of course I probably never would have actually gotten around to it. Eh, maybe we should just be happy for the little gifts the universe gives us.

ENEMIES FOREIGN AND DOMESTIC

My father served in the military. Four years defending our great nation in other countries. Risking his life for the safety and honor of others. When he got home, he trained at the academy and became a police officer in New York, risking his life for the safety and honor of others. Spent the rest of his career battling rapists and thieves and murderers and drug dealers and politics and red tape and protestors who spat on him for things he didn't do. But he hung in there, putting himself in harm's way every day, just to have the courts send the criminals he'd arrested back out on the street over some stupid technicality or because the prisons were getting too crowded. After he retired, he told me the difference between what he did for a living and what he did overseas. He said that when he was fighting over there, at least it was easier to know who the enemy was.

FIRST DATES

First dates have always been awkward for me, so please, forgive me if I say anything inappropriate. I get nervous and sometimes things pop out of my mouth that I didn't even know were in my head. Damn you look good, by the way. Oh, crap, there we go. See what I mean? I'm sorry. What I meant to say was . . . damn you look good. I mean, you're so freaking hot. I mean, have you seen our waiter? I hear this restaurant has the best meat. Beefsteak. Food. Good reviews on the food here. Could we order some wine? Uh, more wine? Maybe not. Maybe I should go. I need to go check on my dog. I don't have a dog. I have a fish. Goldfish. A box of goldfish. Crackers. No, I ate those last night. Waiter! Can we get some breadsticks over here? So, do you get physical on the first date? That was not in my head, I do not know why that came out of my mouth. Is there . . . is there going to be a second date?

AGORAPHOBIA

It's a big bad world out there, Sammy. I don't know if I'm ready to brave it again just yet. Nothing good ever comes of it. And don't you try to tell me any different. I watch the news. I know what goes on out there. People killing each other for drugs, for money, just for the fun of it. Then there's the diseases they spread. Everyone coughing and sneezing and nobody covering their mouths or washing their hands. And if the criminals and the germs don't get you, there's the poisons in the air from the greedy corporations who don't care that they're killing the very same people who are buying their products and keeping them in business. It's stupid. There's a big dark cloud of stupid that hangs over all our heads, and one day it's going to descend on the planet and end us all. Until then, I'm staying safe and snug right here inside my house. Hey, you washed your hands before you came in here, right?

ON CANVAS

I had a pet project. An oil painting I'd been working at on and off for years. It was a landscape. The park where Julie and I met back in college. I'd keep adding things. Falling leaves. Birds. A squirrel. Splinters of sunlight creeping through the trees. I dabbled for so long, I didn't think I'd ever finish it. Then Julie was diagnosed four years ago. Made me promise that no matter what, I would finish the painting. Six months later she was gone. Last year I pulled my unfinished painting out of storage and went back to work on it. I recalled her and I sitting next to each other on a park bench the day we'd met. I brushed us onto the canvas and laid down my palette. I'd finished. I'd added the only thing that was missing. The only thing that was needed. Us. How do you like that, huh? I finally get it right, and she's not here to see it.

VOICES

I hear dead people. No, not like in that M. Night Shyamalan movie. People from my past whose voices I can't get out of my head. Teachers and parents and old bosses. People who stood over me, supervising, criticizing, telling me all the things I was doing wrong. I'm talking about voices from people who have been dead for years, some for decades, still nagging at me. I can hear them like they're standing right there in the room. I tell them to shut up, and they keep yacking. "Oh, you're so inept. How long's it going to take you to catch on to this? I learned better than that my first day. You're useless." Shut up. Shut up. Shut up. I know they're not there. I just wish I could get the memories of them to leave me the hell alone. Every mistake I make, they're bouncing around in my brain, reminding me how incapable I am of doing anything right. Yeah, well, I must be doing something right. I'm still alive. Take that, voices.

FIRST BIKE

I remember my first bicycle. Purple, banana seat, high-rise handlebars. Rode it like a champ until the day my dad took the training wheels off. I climbed on and launched myself from the top of the driveway to get some good momentum going. Figured once I had some speed behind me the balance part would work itself out on its own. I made a left at the sidewalk, forgot to lean in, and instantly became one with the concrete. I laid there crying for what felt like three days. I'm sure now it was no more than a couple of minutes. My mom watched through the living room window, wanting to come out and pamper me. Dad told her to stay put. Said I needed to toughen up. I know that because she told me about it after he'd gone to work. I don't know if she told me because she thought I needed to know that my dad wanted me to learn to get back up on my own after a fall, or because she felt guilty for not disobeying him and coming to my rescue. I never did get around to asking her.

SEEDS OF DOUBT

Don't act surprised when he doubts your sincerity. You're telling him what you think he wants to hear, and he knows it. You're not telling him the truth. You've strayed more than once. Maybe not physically. I don't know, maybe you have. But emotionally, lustfully, I know you have. You've told me on more than one occasion about the fantasies you've had about multiple men at the office. Believe it or not, it's not just your skin he wants. He wants your mind. Your honest affection. Your undivided attention. He really does love you, whether you're worthy of that or not. But he sees you for what you are, and that's killing him. Just because you haven't been cheating with your body, that doesn't make up for being unfaithful in your heart. When you're lying together at night, and he's gazing into your eyes, searching for your soul, who are you seeing when you look into his? I'll bet he knows you're seeing someone else.

PATIENCE

I let you down. I'm so sorry. I know there's no excuse. But, I was preoccupied with work and grocery shopping. I had to take the car in for an oil change. It was almost a thousand miles overdue. Then I stopped for lunch at that new burger place at the mall and spilled ketchup on my shirt, which reminded me I still hadn't picked up my dry cleaning from last week. Then there was an accident on I-94. That took another ten minutes to get around. And it wasn't until I walked in the front door and saw you sitting there waiting for me so patiently that I realized what I had done. I am so sorry, Bruno. You've been so good and so patient, and Mommy forgot to stop at the pet store and buy your treats. Do you forgive me? Does it help if I scratch your ear? Who's Mommy's good boy? Who's Mommy's good boy? You are. You are. That's right. Now stay. I'll go get your treats right now. Mommy will be right back.

FLOWERS FOR BUNNIES

The lady next door and I got into a bit of a spat a few weeks ago. She said she shot rabbits in her back yard for eating her flowers. I told her to plant lettuce. She obviously prized her petunias more than the lives of those cute little bunnies. I found that despicable. So every day since then, I've bought a new cement rabbit from the landscaping place down the road and placed it in my yard, just inside the lot line, facing in her direction. My own little cottontail army to sit and stare her down, day in and day out. I did that to test whether or not she had a conscience. Well, that, and maybe just to piss her off. Anyway, they must have had some kind of effect. Yesterday, while I was at work, apparently she'd snapped, grabbed her rifle, and taken out every one of my cement rabbits and the tires of three of our neighbors' cars. When I got home, the cops were taking her away and I had a mess of cement bunny parts to clean up. But at least now the real bunnies can have all the flowers they want.

HERE'S A TISSUE

Would you like a tissue? Here, you look like you could use a tissue. Your eyes are getting that about-to-weep film over them. Is your nose starting to get that pre-cry tingle? Getting a lump in your throat? Come on, you act like you didn't see this coming. Did you really expect any outcome other than this one? When you stepped out and started seeing Bobby behind my back, did you honestly think I'd never find out? No, I don't buy it. You may be dumb, but you're not stupid. We've watched the same reality shows together. The Jerry Springer crap. Divorce Court. Hell, your brother-in-law is a private detective. You couldn't possibly think this wasn't going to get back to me. But then, how could you have known the girl working the front desk at the Day's Inn was a good friend of mine from high school? You couldn't. But look at the bright side. You and Bobby can be together full time now. So here, take this box of tissues, dry those fake puppy-dog eyes, and run along. Because I'm done with you.

JUSTICE

Yes, part of me wants to end you right here and now. A big part of me. Some people would call that justice. Some would call it flying off in a mindless rage and tearing a murderer to pieces before the judicial system was allowed to do its job. But if I did that, your suffering would be over and I'd be the one defending myself in court. And that just wouldn't be right. So I'm going to show you a mercy you didn't extend to your victims. I'm going to show you that I have something you don't. Restraint. As badly as I want to, I'm not going to put a bullet in your head. I'm not going to beat you to death. I'm going to take you in and let the whole world watch as you go on trial for your crimes and get sentenced to life in prison and hopefully get a taste of your own medicine every day for the rest of your miserable damn life. I'm hoping that will bring at least a little peace to the families of the people you've abused and killed. I know it'll make me feel better.

STAR ATHLETE

I had big dreams. I was going to go all the way. I was looking forward to getting offers from all the big franchises. Multi-million dollar contracts, buying a new home for my parents, being world famous, the whole deal. My friends knew I was going to make it, too. Had myself an athletic scholarship to State. The week before I left for college they decided to throw me a party. We all got together at Jim's parents' house while they were away and had a major blast. There was alcohol, and they wanted me to drink with them, but I refused. I wasn't going to let anything stand in the way of my career. A couple of the guys got drunk and thought it would be funny to tackle me on the living room floor when I wasn't looking, just so one day they could say that they took down the star athlete. We fell on the coffee table, my leg broke in three places, and my ankle was crushed. Yeah, they took me down, all right. Now I'm working the cash register at Kohl's.

PLAYING CHECKERS

The corporate world? The big city? It's not a jungle out there. It's brick and it's concrete and it's glass and metal and flesh and bone and anger and conflict and there's too much of all of it. And if I don't take a break from it . . . I'm going to succumb to its influence and become part of the problem. I'm going to start dishing out some of what this society has been inflicting on me, and I don't want to do that. I don't want to become that person. I'd rather be part of the solution, but I'm about at the end of my rope, and I'm thinking I've got two options here: stay where I'm at and keep doing what I'm doing and wait for something inside me to snap and cause me to do something I'll regret and can't take back, or relocate to some little farm town in the boonies, open a small hardware store, and live out the rest of my days playing checkers and selling rakes and hammers and manure. I'm thinking that's got to be better than the shit I'm dealing with here.

TAKING IT WELL

I'm not taking this well? I'm not taking this well? You're damn right I'm not taking this well. You just fired me. Who takes that well? Anyone? Ever? I've dedicated the last five years of my life to making sure this company made a profit. That this department always stayed productive and under budget. What about Stephens? He hasn't met his quotas in months. I don't see you firing him. Or Collins. He's the laziest son of a bitch in the office. Empties the coffee pot every morning by ten, never brews a new one. I bring in doughnuts every Tuesday. Every. Damn. Tuesday. Who else here does that? You want to know? I'll tell you. No one. Hey, you know what? Fine. I'll take this well. I'll lower my voice, I'll be calm, I'll even stretch out a little smile for you here as I'm carrying out this cardboard box of *my* personal belongings from *my* desk. And I hope whoever gets *my* job after I'm gone appreciates the disloyalty this company shows its employees. And I'm keeping the box. *My* box.

DISAPPROVAL

You don't have to voice your disapproval of me for me to know how you feel. Even aside from the corner of your mouth pinching up, your eyes squinting, your forehead tightening, you're already telegraphing it pretty well. The crossed arms, the tilted head, unnecessary. The air in the room is thick enough without all the posturing. I'm quite aware that you've never approved of me. I don't know what, if anything, I've said or done to offend you, but I've grown to not care. If you didn't want me to marry your father, you should have said something a long time ago. Not that it would have made a difference, but at least it would have been out in the open sooner. But now that it's done, and now that we've both made our positions quite clear, I believe we should both, from here on out, keep our opinions to ourselves and try to make the best of the situation. So no, you don't have to say what's on your mind. In fact, I'd really rather you didn't.

BROWN BAGGING IT

Marty decided to take lunch the other day. Actually, he decided to take someone else's lunch—out of the fridge at work. Mine. I pack my own lunch every day. Usually a sandwich. Just bologna, cheese, and mayo. I leave it in the fridge in a brown paper bag with my name on it. Simple, saves money, and gives me more time to relax while I'm on break. Except when Marty steals it and eats it before I can get to it at noon. I approached him about it a couple of times, but he always denied it was him. So one day last week, instead of mayo, I slathered a heap of wasabi sauce on the sandwich. Marty came flying out of the breakroom, hand over his mouth, Niagara Falls pouring from his eyes. He took the afternoon off. When I saw him the next day, I asked him what had happened. He mumbled something about allergies. Pollen. After giving me a very dirty look, that is. I don't think he was very happy with me. But hey, my lunch hasn't gone missing since.

COUNT ON YOU

Now you listen up, young lady. Nobody ever said life was going to be pretty, and they were right not to. It's hard enough for a man with money and a good background to make it out there. And a man without those things has it even harder. But you're a girl. You've got no worries right now, but when you get older, when you're a woman and you have to find a way to put a roof over your head and food in your belly, you're going to find that it can be pretty damned difficult. But you can do it. I see it in you. You just have to plan. Use your brain. Work hard. And don't you dare for one minute count on finding some man to carry you through life, no matter what any of them might promise. They're not reliable. And they're only out for themselves. You've got to count on you. You go out and make a place in this world for yourself, 'cause ain't nobody gonna give you nothin'. And if they do, it's only because they're wanting more in return than you need to be giving.

TRUCE

I spotted him through the smoke and the breaks in the concrete walls that had somewhat survived the mortar fire. Not wanting to lose sight of him and not wanting to stumble over rubble and bring attention to myself, I chose to stay hidden and quiet. Wait him out. Let him come to me. I blinked and he was gone. Sneaky little bastard ducked behind something. I couldn't see him, so I closed my eyes and focused on listening. I knew he'd be listening too, so I tried not to breathe. It felt like two hours, but it couldn't have been more than a minute, I'm sure. Then I heard a boot stepping on some debris about ten feet behind me. I spun and aimed my weapon. He was standing there, holding a bayonet, looking just as terrified as I was. I could have told him to leave. That there was no need for further bloodshed. That we could call a truce between us and both just walk away. I could have.

EXPECTATIONS

One day, we'll live in a perfect world where fast food restaurants get our burger orders right the first time, telemarketing auto-dialer machines are outlawed, and grocery store stock boys learn to fill the shelves without destroying the products with their box cutters first. Where young people being employed for the first time don't have to be taught how to smile and give friendly customer service, because their parents instilled them with proper communication and social skills before sending them out of the home to get adult jobs. But until then, we'll just have to settle for the imperfect lives we're living now. You'll have to contend with people like me. People who expect those around them to show a little respect, to do their jobs, to actually take a little pride in their work and do the things their employer expects them to be able to do. And until then, people like me will have to suffer through dealing with people like you, who miserably fail to live up to the expectations of people like me. Punch out, go home, and don't come back. You're fired.

ALL ON MY OWN

I never had any help from my parents, my friends, my school counselors. If I wanted anything I had to go out and get it. I've worked hard all my life. Paper route, delivered pizzas, mowed lawns, whatever I had to do to put myself through college. Got a job at an investment company, learned the ropes, and eventually taught myself how to fight hard, go for the throat, and not care that my gain was some other poor sucker's loss. I flushed my soul down the toilet and got rich doing it. I made a life for myself, all on my own. And therein lies the rub. All on my own. I missed my high school proms. I never got married. Never had a relationship long enough to even think about getting married. But that's okay. I don't need a doting mate to tell me I've made it. I've got my bank account to tell me that. And I got that all on my own. All by myself.

REAL MONSTERS

I'm sorry. All this time I thought you were behind this. Granted, I think my suspicion was warranted with all the things you have done, but I should have known this was beneath even you. Your mother, though. Sweet old Betty? Who would have suspected? Starting rumors, making accusations, spreading them around town so people would think I was an abusive parent. All so your family could have bogus ammunition to use at the custody hearing. Then Betty starving Lucy when she was watching her, pushing Lucy down and scraping her head on the cement, just so she could accuse me of mistreating her. And you never said a word in my defense. You know damn well I would never hurt our daughter. I'm just glad your mother's nosey neighbor chimed in and told the police what really happened before they took me to court. So I'm sorry I pointed the finger at you. In this case, your mother was the real monster. But at least now we know where you get it from.

WORLD PEACE

Things were different back then. You and I were different. We both had plans on how we were going to change the world. We were going to replace apathy and world hunger with compassion and world peace. Government would cave to our rebellion and corporate politicians would be tossed into the streets when we voted in the independent candidates who would push our agendas and do all the right things for all the right reasons. But somewhere in there, our message got lost. Jobs and bills and family and the weight of the world bogged us down. And all that passion we had for the future slowly faded away. I want to say that I'd give anything to get that passion back, but I honestly can't remember what it felt like or why it went away. Maybe it was too overwhelming to last. Maybe us being that emboldened wasn't meant to carry over into adulthood. But I look at the world we live in now, and I do wish we'd been more successful with our rebellion.

HIDING PROBLEMS

Have you noticed that Rebecca has been wearing the same outfit every day this week? I thought at first she was just weird or had a closetful of the same clothes. Of course I didn't say anything to her about it. I didn't want to embarrass her. But I also noticed that she's been really quiet lately. I mean, more so than usual. She's always pretty much kept to herself, but recently she's been nearly mute, not even making eye contact. I talked to Wally in human resources. He said to keep it on the hush because he wasn't supposed to be saying anything, but, last week, Rebecca's house burned down. She lost everything. The only clothes that didn't get burned up were the ones she was wearing at the time. Wally said she's been living in a motel over on Eighth. I want to help her, but I can't let her know I know anything. I'd get Wally in trouble. I guess you never know what other people are going through.

BUBBLE GUM

Liz and I were best friends since we were kids. Always enjoyed each other's company. We were complete dorks, both of us. But she never made fun of me and I never made fun of her. Well, that's not entirely true. There was that one time when she stuffed four pieces of bubblegum in her mouth and blew a bubble so big that when it popped it got all in her hair. After I got done laughing, we used peanut butter, olive oil, ice. Whatever we could find to try to get the gum out before her mom saw her. I think we just made it worse. Her mom took her to the barber the next day and she got a boy's haircut. The other kids laughed at her, but I told her it was a brave new look, and that she should be proud to sport something so different and cool. The style actually came into fashion a few years later. Not because of her, I'm sure, but it did make her feel better. I asked that they give her that same haircut before they laid her to rest last year. Yeah, Liz always was ahead of her time.

ADDICTION

You obviously don't want help. You're an addict. And you'll never not be an addict. You enjoy it too much. You enjoy the drugs. You enjoy your little escapes from reality. From responsibility. You thrive on the conflict your lifestyle creates. The adrenalin of watching your family members constantly yelling at each other because of you. You stir the pot in your own little Jerry Springer show. You love being the center of attention. And when you're not the center of attention, you show up high and crying and lying about somebody abusing you. No, you'll never be cured of your addictions. You don't want to be cured. You're addicted to being an addict and you will be until the day you die, which may not be much longer if you keep this up. Call me if you're ever serious about wanting help.

BEING RESPONSIBLE

I didn't think I was ready for this. It's something we're brought up to look forward to, and when it comes, you're somewhere between excited and terrified. And the future is such a blur. All of a sudden you're forced to be responsible, you have to make so many plans, make sure your finances are in order, change your life completely. Suddenly your time isn't your own anymore. Nothing is your own anymore. Everything revolves around someone else. Someone who depends on you every minute of every day for their survival. And it scares you to death, because you don't know if you're up to the challenge. But then the big day comes, and your baby arrives, and you hold her tiny little body in your arms, and you know that this is why you're here. Everything has lead up to this moment. To bringing another life into this world. And you're filled with so much joy, you can't imagine making any other choice but this one.

MIND CONTROL

Yes, I signed his release. I saw no reason to keep him at the facility any longer. He told me the episodes had stopped. He was taking his medication on his own and he appeared emotionally stable. When he showed up at my office on Thursday, he was distracted, out of sorts. Delusional. He was experiencing hallucinations. He kept looking out the window and talking frantically about government agents with mind control technology that were hunting him down. Said they were in league with an alien queen that had come from Venus to take over the planet and he was the only one who could save us. Said he had proof. I asked to see it. So he took me to his car. He popped the trunk, and there was that woman who'd been reported missing on the news. She was barely recognizable. Not as that woman . . . as a human. Apparently, he hadn't stopped hitting her after she was dead. I'm sorry I released him from the hospital. It's pretty obvious now . . . he wasn't ready.

LIVE LONG AND PROSPER

All our married lives, I assumed that my wife thought that shows like *Star Trek* were for kids from the sixties and geeks who went to comic book conventions and still lived in their mothers' basements. When I watched television by myself I was all over the sci-fi and oldies channels. But whenever I heard her coming toward the family room, I'd always switch to something I knew she liked. Like local news or the Learning Channel or the History Channel. Or one of the court shows. I know she watched a lot of those home improvement shows. You know, the ones where they buy houses, do major renovations, then flip them for a profit. Yeah, well, I went to the store for beer one day, and when I got home, she had fallen asleep in front of the television. On the screen, hundreds of tribbles were falling from a storage bin and landing on Captain Kirk's head. My wife and I had a long discussion after that. Then we went to the local geek shop and bought his and hers Starfleet shirts and all three seasons of the original *Star Trek* series on DVD.

BRAVE FOOL

You're one of the bravest men I've ever known. You risked your life to run into a burning building to save complete strangers. You rescued a mother and all three of her children. They're alive today because of you. I'm so proud of you. Everyone is. You're all over the news. The mayor is planning on giving you a medal. As he should. God knows you deserve it. A few, as far as I'm concerned. The fireman I spoke to said that you'd already pulled the family out by the time they'd arrived. He also said you were a fool for rushing into the building like that without any training or protective gear. I told him that yes, you were a fool, but an incredibly brave fool. And now you have to be brave again. I can't imagine the pain you're going through, but you have to be strong. The doctors say you can make it if you just have the will. So please, hang in there. You've been brave for others, be brave for you now.

WAITING IN LINE

I seriously doubt you want to know very much about me. And I can't blame you for that. I'm not a ten. Or a nine. Hell, I'm maybe a seven on a good day. And I'm sure you get more than your fair share of high numbers at any given time. Some of them waiting in line for you. I don't think you even realize how fortunate you are, which could be part of your problem. You don't know how good you have it. What you also don't know is what you're missing here or how good you could have it. You don't know that I am someone you could actually have an intelligent conversation with after sex. That I know respect. That I can listen. That I understand what it means to need companionship or to require space from time to time. That I have so much more to offer than any of your plastic playthings out there. Look, I know I'm no nine or ten, but you could do worse than me. Unfortunately for you, honey, I don't wait in line for anyone.

NO REGRETS

Oh, sure, you would have searched for some alternative to putting an abrupt end to the situation the way that I did. When that man threatened the lives of my wife and children, I could have tried to get a restraining order. I also could have watched my family die while I was waiting for a broken system to try to save them before it was too late. But I went straight to the source. I killed him. With no regrets. My family is safe now. But remember this, the crime of murder isn't always a violent physical act. Sometimes, it's a sentence imposed by twelve people at once when they condemn a man who was justified in his actions. Yes, you can convict me. You can send me away for the rest of my life for doing what you all know damned well you would have done yourself if you'd been in the same situation. If not literally, at least in your heart. So go ahead, pronounce me guilty. Because I'm just like you, and not a one of you is innocent.

HUMORLESS

I get it. You have no sense of humor. But would it kill you to try and recognize that other people do? Come on, just because everyone's laughing in your direction, doesn't mean they're laughing at you. No, actually, let me reassess that. They were laughing at you. And do you know why? It's not because you sat on a whoopee cushion and made those wonderfully hilarious fart sounds. I mean, yeah, that was part of it. Farts are funny. Everyone knows that. Especially when they come from some humorless tight-ass that no one would expect to hear them from. They laughed at you because of the way you reacted to it. Though I must admit the look on your face was priceless. But you acted all pissed off. Like someone dropped a deuce in your cornflakes. If you would've just gone along with the joke and laughed it off, then everyone would've been laughing with you. See how that works? Now, when no one's looking, go and sneak that cushion onto Suzie's chair. Trust me, that'll be some funny stuff right there.

FORCED RETIREMENT

Hey, I'm not happy about this either, Fred. I'm really not. I'd hoped we could have held on longer. Had time to develop a better working relationship. I think we could have done well together. But if this company is going to survive, there are going to have to be some changes made, starting at the top. The board already decided. I'm sorry. It was unanimous. But look at it this way, Fred, you started the company. You've put in your time. You did quite well for yourself. Now it's my turn to take the wheel and see where I can steer this ship. It's a new day, Fred. We need new blood. Fresh ideas. I know I can make things happen here. Hey, look. You're lucky. No more early morning grind at the office. No more high-pressure meetings or piles of paperwork on your desk. Go on, take in some fresh air. Spend more time with the grandkids. You've got one hell of a retirement package. You know, honestly, I just hope when I'm your age, I get the same deal.

NO SECOND PLACE

My grandpa Henry died a couple years back. Heart attack. I never thought anything would beat him. The guy was a bull. I remember when I was young he'd arm wrestle all the kids on the block. He'd drag it out and grit his teeth and act like he was about to give in, right before he took you down. Gave you just a little bit of confidence so you'd think if you worked on it, maybe next time you could beat him. He was the one who always told me not to hold back on anything. Ever. That whatever I had in mind to do, I should do it full force, head on, with every ounce of energy and every bit of strength I had, or not at all. I think he was the first one to tell me that winning second place meant that you were the first one to lose. At least he practiced what he preached. He challenged me to a footrace through the park one day. He put his whole heart into it, just like always. Never gave up. But this time his heart gave up on him.

THANKFUL

You know, I've been complaining for years about everything. My job, rush-hour traffic, the idiots who can't get a damned hamburger order right, my parents, your parents, our neighbors. Of course you know that. You've been listening to me complain all this time. And you stood by me, patiently listened, and never contradicted me. I know you must have opinions of your own. I've just been so busy bitching I don't think you've been able to get a word in edgewise. I'm sorry. Really. I mean, I'm not sorry for all the things I've said about all those people who pissed me off. I'm sorry I haven't taken the time to listen to you. As much as this world angers me, I have to remember that I do have plenty to be thankful for. I have you. I seem to keep forgetting that. So if there's anything you'd like to say, I'm all ears.

EMPTY CANS

When I woke up this morning and tried to roll out of bed, well, off the couch, I thought we had gone to war. I heard metal popping all around me. I jumped up and almost killed myself tripping over all the empty beer cans. Some smartass at the party had piled a few dozen of them on me after I'd passed out. Judging from the massive pounding in my head, I'd guessed that all those empty cans were mine. I had to guess, because I certainly couldn't remember. Hey, it was a party, and I wasn't the only one drinking my ass off. Since I was the first one in the room to come out of my coma, all the noise I'd made woke up the other four people who were passed out around me. We were all complete strangers. I spoke up first. I asked if anyone there knew whose house we were in. They all shook their heads. Then one of them pointed at me and asked if I knew where my pants were. And by the way, no, I didn't.

I TOLD YOU

You never listened to me. You never believed I had your best interests in mind. You thought I was trying to work some angle on you to keep you from competing with me. You had to know there was plenty out there for the both of us. That's not why I was trying to get you to back off. I'm not greedy. But they are. You go stepping on the wrong toes, you're gonna get hurt. Especially those toes. Those boys are family. They don't play around. They're all about serious business. But you thought you could play an end run, sneak around, and make yourself a big score without anyone noticing. Why do you think I turned you down when you asked me to partner with you? I told you a stunt like that would get you killed, and now look at you. Damn it, man, why didn't you listen to me? What am I gonna tell your wife and kids?

MASKS

I understand where you're coming from, I really do. He seemed like the perfect man at first. Good looking, kind, funny, romantic. All those masks we wear when we first meet someone and we want to put our best foot forward. Make that great first impression. We all do it, you know that. Then, after a while, the novelty wears off and the real us starts slipping through. But by the time the masks disappear, it's too late, we're already hooked. And when things aren't as we expected them to be, we want to fix them. Ending the relationship and going out to resume our search for the perfect mate is too much trouble. It's easier to just get this one to change, right? You know what I'm saying. You can fix him. You'll make it work. Well guess what, honey? We are what we are. He is what he is. Trust me, he's not going to change. Either love him for what he is, or go back out there and start over.

DEER IN THE HEADLIGHTS

Stay focused. Look at me. Right here. We're gonna get through this. I've never lied to you, I'm not about to start now. Say, that was one gorgeous deer, wasn't it? Close call. When she stopped right in front of you I thought for sure she was going to be roadkill. But you swerved just in time. Lightning reflexes. I'll bet her babies are grateful to you for not hurting their mama. Boy, we're gonna have one great story to tell when this is over, that's for sure. Keep your eyes open. Look at those trees. Beautiful, aren't they? Yeah, the car doesn't look so good though. I think it's going to take more than a little touchup paint to fix that mangled mess. Those roadside flowers are pretty. Smell nice, too. Breathe them in. Breathe out. Stay awake. Just keep breathing. Wait. Listen. Can you hear that? I hear an ambulance coming. We're gonna make it. Just keep holding my hand. I got you.

NOT GOING TO GRIEVE

I'm supposed to be solemn? Like I'm sorry he's dead? Why is it that when someone who has been a jackass all his life dies, suddenly, he's no longer a jackass? When you stop breathing, all your sins are absolved? Every obnoxious thing you've ever done, every stupid statement you've ever made just magically disappears? All the people you've hurt with your words or your actions are miraculously healed once you're dead? No. It doesn't work that way. The damage that's been done isn't wiped away in the absence of the abuser. I had dreams. Goals. He took those things away from me. His drinking caused my mother to leave. His gambling burned up the money that was supposed to put me through college. Then he goes and dies and leaves me nothing to live on? The man was a jackass in life, and he'll be a jackass for all eternity. I refuse to grieve.

INTOLERANT

I told my son that boys don't kiss boys. That it was just wrong, and never mind all the teasing he would get at school about it, if he ever kissed a boy and I found out, I'd lay a beating on him so bad that he would wish he'd never even heard the word *gay*. I tried to raise him right. I don't know what I said or did that made him go in that direction, but he went. He went, all right. As soon as he was old enough, he went right on out of my life and didn't come back. That was two years ago. Mrs. Barrick from down the block brought me the newspaper last week. Showed me the wedding announcement. My boy and a buddy of his from high school decided to get married two states over where that kind of thing goes on all the time. Where people don't seem to care much who gets married to whom. I don't know how the hell I'm supposed to have grandkids. Hell, I'm thinking I don't know much of anything these days.

SEEN A GHOST

Have you ever seen a ghost? No, really. Have you? Because I know they don't exist, but I could swear I saw one yesterday. You know that Henry in accounting is getting married to the boss's daughter, right? Well, of course Henry wants to appear worthy and proper for his soon-to-be father-in-law, so apparently he decided to let go of his beloved porn collection. Boxed it all up and put it to the curb for the morning's trash pickup. Unfortunately for him, the truck was late and a couple of his groomsmen, whom he shouldn't have told about the magazines, heisted the box and brought it to the office. They stacked all his *Chic*, *Adam*, *Penthouse*, *Gallery*, and *Hot Asian Babes* mags in a pyramid on the conference table right before he arrived for the morning meeting. Henry stepped into the room, took one look at the pile, and I swear, his jaw dropped and his face turned as white . . . yeah . . . as white as a ghost. Funniest part is, the boss was in on it.

FINE PRINT

That's how they get you, you know. They hypnotize you. They pop something on the screen to catch your attention. A sharp-looking woman in a bikini, an old couple on a roller coaster, a building exploding. Anything to grab you and pull you in. And once they've got you, bam, bam, bam. Every half second, one shot after another of people having a great time using their product, inundating you with subliminal messages of buy me, buy me, buy me. And for the love of Pete, don't even think about pulling out your magnifying glass and trying to read the fine- fine- fine- fine- print disclaimers for the brief moment they flash at the bottom of the screen. No time for that. Look, look, look. The old woman who took her vitamins is skydiving. The bald guy selling scalp tonic now has a full head of hair. The pimple-faced teenager is being hit on by a seductive cougar thanks to his new body spray. Always keeping your attention away from those disclaimers. Skin rash, achy joints, kidney failure, heart attack, cancer. And you buy what they're selling, because hey, the commercials make their products look so unbelievably good. And that's how they get you.

NOTHING I CAN DO ABOUT IT

Don't even try to tell me you've never been helpless. Everyone has been at least one time, a dozen times, maybe hundreds of times in their lives, to some degree. But totally, unquestionably, stupidly helpless? At least once. And this is my once. Totally, unquestionably, stupidly helpless. That's me right now. I've been in love before, or thought I had. But not like this. Not a love that had me so confused and so focused at the same time. So drunk and so sober. It's like my life is a massive blur, and the only thing coming through as clear as day is you. You took everything I've ever known about love and pushed it aside and replaced it with a miraculous vision that has shown me what I've been missing all along and never knew. That you really are the center of my universe. I'm helpless. I love you. I love you, and there's not a damn thing I can do about it.

REPEAT OFFENDER

I have better places to be and better things to do than to hang around here trying to fix your problems. How many times have I bailed you out now? I've lost count. And you keep pulling the same crap over and over again? You obviously haven't learned from any of this. Look, I'm not the one who broke into that liquor store, got drunk, passed out, and didn't wake up until the police arrived. This was all you, buddy. I always knew you weren't the sharpest cookie on the shelf, but this was just plain stupid. If you're going to steal booze, wait until you get home to drink it. At least then you could have shared it, you wouldn't have gotten so obliterated, and I wouldn't have had to take the morning off work to come see you in jail. Since you wasted your phone call on me, I'll call an attorney for you, but don't expect any help paying his fees. Not from me. Your father and I are done. We can't afford you anymore. Financially or emotionally.

SPACE AND TIME

I need time. How much time? I don't know in minutes or hours or days, I just know I need time. Time to sort things out in my head. You tell me that you want to be with me, then you tell me I'm smothering you. You need your space. So I give you space. I back off. I give you all the room you need, because for goodness' sake, I certainly don't want you to resent me for trying to spend time with you. Then you complain that I've given you too much space. That you're lonely. You want me to be with you more. Well, to be with you more takes time. Time I've recently been putting into figuring out what I was going to do next in my life since I had obviously been encroaching too much on your time. But now, working on my life is supposed to be put on hold because you don't need your space anymore. Well, guess what? I do. And I need time. Time to consider if this relationship is the healthiest thing for me.

MODERN FORENSICS

Eric should realize something; today's modern forensic technology is saving his life. With fingerprinting and DNA and massive database cross-referencing and all the combined sciences that go into solving crimes nowadays, it's very difficult to get away with murder anymore. It used to be that you could shoot someone in the head, place the weapon in their hand, call it suicide, and walk away. That was before they thought to check for gunshot residue. Clean up that blood. Scrub it out of the carpet. Make it look like new, and no one will ever guess you gutted someone there the week before. But Luminol makes the unseen particles of blood glow like a full moon and now you're a prime suspect. I'll bet you if murder wasn't so hard to get away with because of all these advancements in forensic science, a lot more people would be doing it. I would be, that's for sure. So yeah, Eric should be grateful for the progress forensic science has made. It keeps me from taking my revenge on him for stealing Angela from me.

FORGIVENESS

I screwed up. Over and over again. I just couldn't seem to get this whole relationship thing right. I can't say for sure how sincere I was about it, but I apologized every time. And the amazing thing was, she kept forgiving me. She kept telling me I was human, and that humans make mistakes. The more I screwed up, the more I apologized. And the more she forgave me, the more I wanted to be a better person. But being a screw-up is in my blood. Either I'd forget her birthday, fail to compliment her or comfort her when she really needed it, or just inadvertently say something stupid and insensitive, trying to be funny. I wasn't funny, I was just dense. Stupid. And apparently there is some mathematical equation that we screw-ups are oblivious to that's used to calculate the quantity of screw-ups that leads to the crossing of a line someone we care about has drawn. I crossed that line, I guess. If I want to be forgiven now, I'll have to find a way to forgive myself.

FAVORITES

I stopped by the home to see dad today. He's not looking so good. He's deteriorating fast. But during the moments that he's lucid enough, he asks about you. I'm running out of excuses for why you're not going to see him. Why can't you go? Just once? Look, I know you always said that I was his favorite, but I really think that was more your perception than his. I never saw it. I always thought he would rather be with you, but he spent more time with me because I needed it more. You were more independent. You always have been. But whatever you thought was going on back then, you gotta get past it. That was a long time ago. Dad wants to see you. If you put it off much longer it's not going to matter. He's going to stop asking about you. Not because he doesn't care or because he doesn't love you. It's just not going to be that much longer he'll be able to remember either of us. You've been a stranger to him for years. Don't wait until he doesn't recognize you to visit him.

GRATITUDE

Thirteen years, in case you're wondering. Four years of undergraduate study, four years of medical school, and five years of surgical residency. During that time I studied anatomy, microbiology, biochemistry, physiology, pathology, psychology, ethics, medical law, and a fat handful of other things. I've been a licensed surgeon for twelve years now, and I haven't lost a patient yet. I consider that a pretty damned good record. If I hadn't performed that surgery on you, you would have shriveled up and died within the next three months. So do you have any idea how it makes me feel when you thank God for saving your life, when it was my talent, my expertise, my training, my experience, and my steady hands that saved you? Go ahead, thank God one more time. I dare you. I'll wheel your ass back down the hall and put that tumor of yours right back where I found it. So when you finally get around to showing some real gratitude and giving credit where credit is due . . . you're welcome.

GUSTO

All it takes is one stupid mistake. One little misstep and it's all over. Look left when you should have looked right. Zig when you should have zagged. Look at Christopher Reeve. A good man who had everything going for him. On top of the world. A great acting career. A beautiful family. Riding his horse one minute, in a wheelchair the next. For the rest of his life. We're so damned fragile. What the hell would have possessed any creator to make us so easy to break? It's not fair. We're all given the greatest gift, life. Life, something so precious, and yet so easily taken away. So in order to live a good, long life, we have to be careful, walk on eggshells so we don't damage ourselves. But at the same time, what's life if we don't run out there and live it to the fullest? And there's no guarantee either way, that if we're careful we live long or that we won't survive if we choose to go for the gusto. It's all a crapshoot. So, how are we supposed to live our lives? I'm thinking the answer is, however it suits us.

HARD DECISIONS

There are people out there who will instinctively throw themselves in front of a bullet to save another person's life. Without a thought, they will sacrifice everything in a flash, because something inside them at that very moment takes over and tosses self-preservation out the window in favor of protecting a fellow human being. I think that's because we are basically good. And we're of the hive. Survival of the species takes precedence over the needs of the individual. But we ignore our instincts when we're given time to think about them. Too many of us hold tight to our wallets and choose to not be charitable when we know our charity is needed the most. But we are better than that. We have the power to overcome our selfishness and give of ourselves to those in need. So please, think about it. Don't walk away. My daughter's troop needs your help. Just ask yourself, "Which do I choose, the thin mints, or the peanut butter patties?" And, "Two boxes, or three?"

NOT LIKE THAT

My sister's not like that. She took care of me when I was a kid. She's the one who kept my father from beating me. She'd stand between us and take the punishment herself, so I wouldn't have to. He didn't care who he was beating up on, as long as it was someone smaller and weaker than him. Most of the time he was probably so drunk he didn't know the difference. I don't know who killed my father. Not that I'm that terribly upset about it happening. I know this is wrong to say, but if anyone deserved to die like that . . .

My mother left us when I was five. I guess she'd had enough and ran off to create a new life for herself. My sister was fourteen. She pretty much raised me. She's the one they tried to pin my father's death on. But it wasn't her. She's not like that. She's the kindest, gentlest person you could ever meet. She wouldn't hurt a fly. Unless that fly was about to hurt her little brother.

VOLUNTEER

Do you even know what a volunteer is? A volunteer is someone who agrees to set aside time out of their life to do something that doesn't directly benefit only them. When there is a need to fill an unpaid position, have someone present to man a post, or take on any responsibility to make sure that whatever it is that needs to be done is done, that's where the volunteer comes in. A volunteer is the one who steps up to the plate and says, "Hey, you need someone there to do that thing at that time? Don't worry, I've got you covered." And when that volunteer decides at the last minute that they've suddenly got something more important to attend, like a picnic or a movie, or they just don't feel like following through with their commitment, then they're no longer a volunteer. They're just some jackass who kept something from being accomplished because they didn't stand down and let someone volunteer who knew how to keep a promise. You weren't here, so I had to run out and get the doughnuts myself. Don't volunteer again unless you mean it.

STRAWBERRIES AND HUGS

I was six years old when she died. I still have memories of what she looked like. I don't know if it's because of the pictures my dad kept of her, or if I actually recall seeing her face in person. It's been so long, it's hard to separate the two in my mind. But I do remember strawberries. Not actual strawberries, her hair. She had really long red hair. She always washed her hair in strawberry-scented shampoo. And whenever I was having a bad day, if I fell and hurt my knee, if someone had teased me at school, she would look me in the eye, tell me that everything was going to be okay, and she'd wrap her arms around me and pull me close to her. She'd hold me so tight and her hair would cover my face. And I breathed in . . . peace. Strawberries and hugs fixed everything. That, I do remember. And those are some memories I hope I'll never lose.

COWARDS

Cowards. That's what you are. You're all a bunch of damned cowards. You stood there and watched as a couple of bullies beat up on a weaker kid. Said you didn't want to get involved, but you pulled out your cell phones and video recorded the whole thing. Were you entertained? Did you think it would be fun to post the video on social media and watch the reruns? You know what would have been more entertaining? A few of you cowards stepping forward and protecting the kid who was getting pummeled. But no, you couldn't do that. Because you were cowards. You were afraid the bullies might turn on you. Or worse yet, you were afraid you wouldn't look cool in front of your friends. You were afraid someone would think you were weak for wanting to save a weak kid. But if you had all stepped in together and done the right thing, that would have been real power. The strength of your numbers and of your convictions would have made you all heroes. But no, you didn't want to get involved. Remember that when you're the victim and no one is stepping in to help you.

KILLING IS EASY

In case you've ever wondered, killing someone is easy. Point, pull the trigger, done. Especially when they're posing a threat. A man breaks into your house in the middle of the night. Your wife and kids are sleeping. You pull your revolver from your sock drawer. *Bang.* Dead intruder on your living room rug. That easy. That fast. And you can't feel guilty about it, right? He broke into your house. This guy threatened your home and family. This guy with a pry bar, gloves, and a mask broke in and threatened your home and family. This guy with a wife and three kids, who lost his job six months ago, couldn't find a way out of debt, and in a last ditch effort to put food on the table, made a really stupid choice, broke in, and threatened your home and family. But that was his choice. Not yours. You can't feel guilty about it. He would have done the same to you if you'd broken into his home, right? I mean, his wife, his kids, not your problem, right? You can't feel guilty about it.

LESSONS IN LOVE LOST

If you're going to kill multiple husbands, you have to change your M.O. from one to the next. You've already got the police looking at you for having had more than one spouse kick the bucket on you, you don't need to bring more attention to yourself by having them croak by suspiciously similar causes. You know, like if one falls down the stairs and breaks his neck, maybe the other one gets really drunk and commits suicide. Or if one gets shot in a dark alley, the other gets run down by a stolen car. Whatever the case, make sure you've established good alibis. You gotta think it through, plan far in advance. Wear gloves and be somewhere else when the body is found. And be patient. Put a little time between them. Let the news about your unfortunate loss die down a bit before creating another. Or more to the point, don't kill the second husband while the ink's still drying on the first one's obituary.

PROPAGANDA

I just did what I thought was right. Maybe that's all any of us can strive for—doing what we think is right and hoping that what we think is right, really is right. But how are we supposed to know that for sure? We only know the world from our own narrow perspectives, what we've been taught to believe. But what is fact, and what is propaganda? How do we know we've been given the correct information all our lives? That we haven't been played by the wrong people and unknowingly brainwashed and recruited to the other side? What is the other side? Anyone who isn't us? I thought taking out the enemy was the right thing. It was how we protected ourselves from *them*, whoever *they* are. How we preserved our way of life. The only life we know how to live because we never lived any lives other than our own. I did what I thought was right, what was expected of me. I killed the enemy. The same thing his people expected of him, I suppose.

BIRTHDAY SURPRISE

Let me tell you how I met Jamie, my husband. My first husband, Mark, always liked surprising me for my birthday. He was always coming up with new ideas. Three years ago he built a castle of Twinkies on the dining room table, stuck a candle in the one on top, and invited the whole family to help dismantle and eat it. Two years ago he took me to a comic book convention where he'd prearranged for the Avengers to sing "Happy Birthday" to me. Last year, he hired a stripper to come into our home and perform for me and all the neighbors he'd invited. That stripper was Jamie. We hit it off a little too well. The dance escalated to a performance nobody was expecting, the neighbors got weirded out and left, and Mark and Jamie got into a fist fight. I got in the middle of it and we all spent the remainder of my birthday in jail. The divorce wasn't any prettier. Jamie got me a card and a small cake for my birthday this year. Nice and quiet, just the two of us.

BIG BAD MEN

Why would you go to the media with this? Did you really think that was the right thing to do? This isn't a simple issue for Human Resources, this is dangerous business. Those accounting ledgers were company property, and now that they're public record, there are a number of corporate officers who are probably going to be doing some serious jail time. They're not going to let you get away with this. These are the big boys you're playing with. Once they find out that you're the one who leaked this, they're not going to hesitate to have you done away with. Your testimony in court won't do any good if you're not there to give it because you're encased in cement at the bottom of the river. You may as well just forget about your noble little quest to bring down the big bad men upstairs—you won't see the end of the trial. And you can forget about your life here in the city. If I were you, I'd head out of town, quickly, quietly, and not look back. And I wouldn't stop running.

CHRISTMAS AT THE MALL

I was walking through Northgate Mall last week, doing some last-minute Christmas shopping. I sat on a bench to take a load off and do a little people-watching. This little old lady with a walker slowly made her way over and sat next to me. We talked for a few minutes about the weather, the season, the sales. Nothing huge. Then she excused herself to leave. She starting pulling herself up on her walker, got halfway there, and ripped a fart that got everyone's attention in a thirty-foot radius. She dropped right back down on the bench, embarrassed as hell. Some children walking by pointed and laughed. Some of the parents shooed them along and held back their own giggles. The old woman opened her mouth like she was about to apologize. I winked at her, smiled, leaned sideways, and ripped a stinker of my own. A security guard walking by shook his head at me. The old lady smiled and we high-fived each other. Yeah, I love Christmas at the mall.

DEVIL IN THE DETAILS

You're a slick one, alright. Smooth talker. Not smooth enough, though. There'll be no talking your way out of this one, my friend. You've done everything a man can do to insure his soul is doomed, and yours surely is. We do have an agreement, you recall. You signed it. With your boss's blood. He had that terribly untimely heart attack and you took over his job and no one's challenged you for it all this time. You're welcome. Looks like you've done quite well for yourself. I gotta tell you though, I really think you could have done this without my help. You would have gotten the position eventually. Too bad for you that you were too impatient to wait. But it is what it is. You do what you do and I do, well, you know. It's a *Hell* of a thing, ain't it? It's been ten years. Time to pay up. Besides, I just got another agreement signed. Your protégé wants your position now just as bad as you wanted it back then. Don't bother grabbing your coat, it's pretty warm where you're going.

NEWSPAPERS

Mary hadn't been out of the house in months. Ever since the break-in she's been terrified to open her front door. Stepping outside was definitely out of the question. She did let me in, though. Sometimes. She's known me forever. She used to babysit me when my parents went out to play bingo. I'd been checking in on her from time to time, just to make sure she was okay. Her husband Harold used to read the newspaper. After he died last November, Mary never got around to canceling delivery. I asked her if she wanted me to cancel for her. She said no, that she didn't mind them coming. That they were a comforting reminder of Harold. The papers would pile up on the porch and I'd take them in when I went to see her. She never threw them away. They were stacked in piles all over the house. I drove by the other day, and the house was gone. Burned to the ground. All those newspapers made for good kindling, I suppose. I guess I can tell the paperboy to cancel the subscription now.

UNSUBSTANTIATED RAINBOWS

Please don't stand there and tell me how wonderful things will be in the next world. I can understand looking to the future, but you're grasping at unsubstantiated rainbows. That's far in the future, if it even exists at all. This is the world we're living in here and now, and if you don't focus on getting your life together and finding a way to support yourself, you can definitely forget about the afterlife. For there to be life after life, there has to be life to begin with, and you're letting this one pass you by. Look, I'm not saying to give up all hope of retiring to some utopia after you're dead, I'm just saying maybe you should focus more of your efforts on surviving until then. Hey, here's an idea you might like. As long as you're stuck in that mindset, maybe you could make a living performing séances, telling the future, connecting people with their deceased relatives from the distant beyond. That way you could support yourself while still keeping in touch with your otherworldly vibrations. You know, two birds, one crystal ball.

FOR A SONG

Sadie Jenkins used to live here. Back when her folks had their farm just up the road there. They had a pretty big family and it got a bit crowded there for a while. But, as the kids got older, one by one they'd up and leave town. Some went off to college, some to work in the mill two towns over. But Sadie stayed here. Bought this place for not much more than a song. Took most of what she'd saved up from years of babysitting and making deliveries for Charlie's hardware store, but it was hers and she was proud of it. A couple years ago some James fellow came through town. Got himself a job at Charlie's sweeping floors and stocking shelves. Him and Sadie hit it off right away. Not too long after, they both disappeared and haven't been seen since. Some say it was love. Some say it was something more sinister. Either way, she left the house and everything in it behind. Don't look like she's coming back. So if you're looking to buy the place, you can pretty much have it for not much more than a song.

COMPETENCE

I don't get you. You constantly find ways to sabotage yourself. You and I both know damned well that you are the most competent employee at this company. You know your job better than anyone else here, and that's the only reason they haven't fired you yet. You know you should have been promoted a dozen times by now. You should be running this department. Hell, you should be running the company. But you look for conflict. You find ways to piss off management, and it doesn't matter if you're right or wrong, you just refuse to get along with the people who are in power. I think you resent them so much that you fight advancement, just so you won't become one of them. Well, you know what? I agree with you. You're right. Management is staffed with a bunch of ignorant, stuffed-shirt asshats that all deserve to be fired. But the only way that's going to change is if someone like you is put into a position to do something about it. So, yeah. Make a few concessions now, work your way up, and fix this mess like only you can do.

WORKING TOWARD PEACE

There's a peace we're all hoping to find. An internal peace that the only possibility of achieving is if we can close our eyes and let go of the turmoil that life has plagued us with. One that requires us to forgive ourselves of our past transgressions. To forgive others for the wrongs we've allowed them to inflict on us. A peace that is strong enough to block out all the bad things in the world while being wide open to welcoming in all the good. And if and when we find even just one little sliver of that peace, we need to grab hold of it and hang on with all our might, because if we let it go, there's a possibility we may never see it again. Peace. It's hard. So very hard to find. So very hard to keep. It's a frustrating world out there, and there's a delicate balance between maintaining our sanity and taking the life of some idiot who cuts us off on the freeway. But we work toward peace, because it is essential to our survival. And theirs.

FREEDOM

You're one lucky son of a bitch, Carl. Evidence puts you at the scene of all three rapes. DNA says you're the only suspect. We have three victims. Three damaged women. Three firsthand witnesses who refuse to testify in court because they're afraid of what you'll do to them or their families if they do, mostly because, from what I understand, that's what you threatened them with. Sadly, I can't prosecute you if there are no victims who are willing to press charges, so I can't hold you any longer. You're free to go. You can pick up your personal belongings on the way out. Unless someone gets brave, comes forward, and is willing to identify you in court as the sick bastard who attacked them, I won't be seeing you again. So, good for you, you got away with it. The system worked in your favor today. However, I can't guarantee that there aren't three angry husbands waiting right outside this building to congratulate you on your freedom. Have a nice day, Carl.

BESTSELLING AUTHOR

I don't need to be a bestselling author. I don't have to be famous or make millions of dollars on my writing. I mean, it wouldn't hurt my feelings if those things happened, but that's not what I'm aiming for. It's not like I deserve any of that, anyway. I'm not some literary genius waiting to be discovered. I've got no Earth-shattering message to share with the world. I just want to be recognized for the small amount of talent I think I do have. And I'd like to sell enough copies of my books to make up for all the time I've spent locked away in my home office writing these last ten years while my wife was out making a living and supporting the both of us. I can't go back and start over. That time is lost. But if I could just catch a break and get traditionally published, you know, get some good marketing behind me, maybe I could show her that her belief in my abilities was warranted. That she was right to support my dream. Maybe I should write about that.

REFUSING GOODBYE

I don't want you to leave without me saying goodbye to you first. But I don't want to say goodbye to you. I don't want you to leave. Maybe you don't have a good reason to stay because I haven't given you one yet. But I have one now. A really good one. If you leave me, I won't know what to do with myself. I'll be completely lost. My heart will be broken and I'll be nothing more than a crying mess. I'll spend the rest of my life wondering what I could have done different that would have made you stay. And I'll blame myself and I'll hate myself and I'll be miserable until the day I die. That's a good enough reason, isn't it? I know you. You're a wonderful person. You wouldn't want to be the cause of someone's life completely falling apart. And that's what would happen if you left. Look, I know I haven't lived up to your expectations. I haven't lived up to mine. So I understand if you want to leave. Just please understand why I refuse to say goodbye.

SAYING THE WORDS

No, of course I don't love you. Never did. You've never been anything more to me than a piece of . . . a pain in my ass. But I keep you around because you make good arm candy. I thought you would have figured that out by now. I mean, sure, I want more. Everyone wants more of something. More money, more sex, more . . . more . . . dessert. Not love. Not me, anyway. Not the emotional kind. The physical kind. You know, the kind you can really sink your teeth into without getting caught up in the part that explodes your mind because you're spending every moment of every day trying to figure out what to do or say to make sure someone keeps feeling the same way about you as you do about them. That crap will drive you nuts. But if it would make you feel better, I can certainly say the words. They won't be true. They won't mean anything. But I can say them. I can tell you I love you. Here . . . I love you. Does that make you feel better? Can we get to sleep now?

HUNGRY EYES

I'm telling you, that woman is a psychopath. A lying, thieving, heartless, sadistic psychopath. I guarantee you, anything she told you is a lie. If her lips were moving, a lie. If she said anything nice about me, it was just an effort to sound more credible before setting you up to believe her next onslaught of false accusations. I never touched her. We barely spoke. I could tell right away there was something wrong with her when I first saw her from across the room. She was scanning the crowd, like she was sniffing out her next prey. Her eyes gave her away immediately. Evil. Hungry. Darting. Then when she locked on to me, she flipped the switch from psycho to sweet. But I'd already seen her before the transformation. I already knew what to expect when she approached me, trying to act all coy and sexy. I think the reason she told you all that bullshit about me was because she was pissed off at me for being one of the few men in her life that had the nerve to turn her down.

PERFECT LIKENESS

I was sitting in my home studio, looking at everything I'd drawn in the last five years, sitting on easels, hanging on the walls, stacked on shelves. And I realized something; none of my art was mine. I'd just recreated pencil and ink images of things I saw every day. These were trees, buildings, fountains, things that occurred in nature or were created by other people. Nothing that came from my soul. I'd been too influenced by my surroundings. So I gathered every piece I'd created, and every photo, book, business card, everything but my art supplies, and moved it all to another room. I sat in my studio and soaked in the emptiness. I felt at peace. Calm. Uncluttered. But something was calling to me. One thing I couldn't quite place, and it tugged at the back of my mind. I laid down for a two-hour nap, hoping it would come to me. When I woke, I started randomly drawing. When I finished, the only thing on the paper was a perfect likeness of you.

FAITH

I don't think I care to be a part of this congregation anymore, Father. This church has been my spiritual home for years, but it no longer feels like home. It feels like insecurity and hypocrisy and animosity and apathy. There's just far too much turmoil here. Rumors and secrets and whispers behind closed doors. This used to be the place where my heart felt it belonged. Where my soul knew it could peacefully reside until it was time for me to be laid to rest. I was brought up to believe in this institution and the people who run it just as much as I believe in God. I still have my hopes for mankind. I still think that there's so much more waiting for us when this world has ceased to exist. I still believe in the power of humanity to come to terms with the crimes it has committed against itself and be better than it has been in the past. I still have faith in God. But I can't stay here. Because I've lost my faith in all of you.

INTENTIONS

Look, you and I have been through a lot together. We've known each other too well for too long to try pulling punches. Remember two years ago when you asked your niece's boyfriend about his religious affiliation? And it turned out that you and he both had very strong convictions about your beliefs? He was in the hospital for a week and you went to jail for six months. It's pretty clear that you have restraint problems when it comes to something or someone you care about. And now you're approaching me with this? We both know, if there's a chance you're not going to like the answer, it's probably best to not ask the question. And you know I've always been a straight shooter. I've never lied to you. So please, don't ask me what my intentions are with your sister. My honest response probably won't bode well for either of us. Particularly me.

VICTIM

Please. Please tell me you've got something more to go on. A witness. A security camera. Something one of them left behind. Anything to help catch those bastards. I've given you the best description I could. It was dark. They were wearing ski masks. But they were both talking the whole time they were attacking me. Taunting me, threatening me. Hitting me, kicking me, telling me the whole time that I was going to die. I believed them. I had no reason not to. Even the doctors said it was a miracle I survived. I remember praying through the blood and the pain that they would just kill me and get it over with. Now I pray that you find them and bring them to justice. I didn't see their faces, but I know I'd recognize their voices if I heard them again. Just get them in here, let me hear them. I'll positively identify them. Please. Please don't let them get away with what they did to me.

SENTIMENTAL

Don't get sentimental on me now. You know this hasn't been working out for a long time. I just can't figure out why it took either of us so long to realize it. We've both been working on sabotaging this relationship. I don't know if it died because we didn't know how to save it, or if we both felt it wasn't worth saving, so we intentionally killed it. It doesn't matter. It's over. For what it's worth, I don't hate you. Some part of me still loves you, I suppose. Once love between two people has happened, I don't think that it ever really goes away. Not completely. It's just a shame that it wasn't strong enough to keep us together. Damn, who's getting sentimental now? I'm sorry. Look, thanks for putting up with me for as long as you have, and thanks for all the good memories. I promise I'll keep them for a very long time—whether I want to or not.

NEED TO KNOW

There's something you need to know about your father. He did die, that's true. But he didn't die before you were born. He didn't serve in the military. He was no hero. Far from it. He was a thief. And not a very good one. His last liquor store holdup went all wrong. The owner reached for a gun and your father shot him. He didn't mean to, it just happened so fast he got scared and pulled the trigger. Didn't matter what was going on in his head at the moment, armed robbery and murder meant he was going away for a long time. He died in prison. Two years ago. I could have told you sooner, but he made me promise not to tell you until you grew up and had a career. He thought that if you saw him there you would blame the system for taking your father away. That was on him, and he knew it. He wanted you to focus on your goals. I hope you can forgive me for keeping my promise to him. It was all for you.

TOGETHER

Remember when you and I were fifteen and we jumped the fence at the drive-in theater? We just wanted to see a movie, we didn't care which one. And those other kids had gone in there and vandalized a couple dozen speakers? Something we would never do. You and I got blamed at first, but we hung together and stuck to our guns and eventually the other kids were caught. We got a slap on the wrist and got sent home. Our parents grounded us for a week, but we were fine. We got through it together. Well, guess what? We're together now. We can get through this. I'll do whatever I can to help. I'll visit you every day. I'll bring you that stupid rainbow Jell-O you like so much. I'll sit with you through chemotherapy. Hell, I'll even hold your hair back when you're tossing your cookies, just like I did after you got drunk out of your mind at the prom. And when your hair falls out I'll bring you a wig. Just don't be surprised if it matches your Jell-O. Who else would do all that for you, huh? Hey, I got you. We'll get through this. Together.

IT'S ALL A GAMBLE

I don't think you understand what's going on here. Bob doesn't get you. He really hasn't grasped what you're all about, even though you two have been together for two years. This guy Jim that you met last month at the office Christmas party acts like he's known you all your life and instinctively knows you inside and out like some cosmic soulmate. At least I'm sure that's what he wants you to believe. There are billions of other men on the planet. Most won't truly understand you. Plenty of others will connect with you better than Jim does, and many will be just as clueless as Bob. It's all a gamble, and you won't know if any of those relationships are worthwhile until you've wasted at least some small part of your life investing in them. If I were you, I'd put my money on the guy who's stuck with you through thick and thin. I'd go for the tried and true. I'd look at the person sitting right across the table from me. I'm right here, whenever you're ready.

SAFE DEPOSIT BOX

Look inside the envelope I just gave you. Go ahead. Take a look. You'll find a key to a safe deposit box in Boston, the address of the bank it's in, directions on how to get there, and who to contact once you're inside the bank. They'll be expecting you. In that box are your new driver's license, credit cards, and passport for your new identity. There's also a loaded pistol in there. If you get that far and manage to get all the contents of the box out of the bank without getting yourself caught or killed, you'll need to look over your shoulder for the rest of your life. If any of their agents find you, use the gun on them. If it looks like you're going to be captured, do us all a favor and use the gun on yourself. Trust me, it'll be faster, easier, and much less painful.

MISSION CRITICAL

You must have been pretty desperate to go to this kind of trouble to complete your mission. Waiting until I was out working in the yard. Waiting until everyone else had gone to school or work. I can't imagine how many trips you made from the basement to stack all those boxes up there. How long have you been planning this? I mean, yes, I'm rather upset with you, but I am a little impressed at the same time. This took a good amount of ingenuity on your part. I don't know if I would have come up with anything like this when I was four years old. But you've learned something today, haven't you? Empty cardboard boxes are not Legos. They crush pretty easily under not that much weight. That's why you fell and bruised your knee on the floor. Nevertheless, I must admit, your attempt at creating a staircase to reach the kitchen counter was commendable. I'll make you deal. Go put all these boxes away, promise to not do this again, and the next you want a cookie, all you have to do is ask.

MISTAKES

Yeah, I'm a cop, but I'm also a human being. I make mistakes, just like everyone else. I get emotional. When someone threatens my family, I get angry. I got angry when those two men broke into my house. I knew they were there to kill us, I don't care what anyone else says. I arrested them last month, and they both told me they'd be back. That I'd be sorry. They put me on notice. Sure, I didn't have to empty the clip into them, but damn it they were in my house. I knew what they were there for. I got angry. Excessive force. That's what they're saying. It's all a matter of perspective. I lost my mind. Yeah, I reloaded and shot them again. So what? I wanted to be sure my family was safe. Was that a mistake? Was I wrong to react the way I did? I don't think so. Come on, man. What would you have done?

FORCE OF NATURE

They said it was the cancer that killed her. Twenty years of smoking. Not exercising. Not eating right. But it wasn't any of those things. It wasn't bad cells destroying good cells in her body. It was her attitude. Her death was caused by her outlook on life and how that outlook made her treat other people. Like how she treated me. That's where the dominoes came into play. Her contempt for life and everything around her transferred to me and became my contempt. That transformed into my loathing of her, and that evolved into cosmic forces whipping into a frenzy. She brought out the worst in me, and I sent my worst right back out into the universe, until one day, I was done with her. I'd had enough of the rage that she'd poured into me, and I wanted more than anything for it to end. I balled up all that anger, and with every ounce of my being, I wished her dead. I wished her dead, and the forces of nature complied. It wasn't the cancer. It was me. I killed her, just by wanting it so bad.

EVEN-TEMPERED

My dad called last night. I hadn't heard from him in a couple of months. He's pretty independent. Always has been. When I was a kid he'd always be off working two jobs, keeping himself busy doing pretty much anything to be away from us. That's how I saw it, anyway. I think he justified it by claiming to be the best breadwinner he could be. When he was at home, he was pretty even-tempered. Nothing got him angry or laughing or sad. He always took everything in stride. Even when Mom passed away he was a stone. He just made the funeral arrangements, bought a puppy, and moved on with his life. When I answered the phone last night I heard a quiver in his voice. He told me his little dog had died. Then he bawled like a baby. That was the first time I'd ever heard him cry. As much as I'd always wanted to see any kind of emotion from him, I think I could have gone the rest of my life without hearing that.

CASTING THE ROLE

Why not you? Why not any one of a hundred other women I know or another one of the dozens who auditioned for the role? This is my film. My screenplay. My production. The script only calls for two characters, John and Becky. I wrote the male role for me, and I cast myself. That was the easy one. As for Becky, I had a very specific vision in mind for the female role, and I'm sorry, but you didn't fit that vision. I developed that role on paper as having a complex set of characteristics, and I needed someone who could capture the essence of Becky, and that someone was Lisa. Not just because she looks the part, but because she has the skillsets needed to bring real believability to the role. She brings the character to life in a way that I couldn't even see myself when I created Becky. So I'm sorry I couldn't cast you, but no matter who got the role, there would still be a million other actors who didn't. That's just how it works.

DANGEROUS MISSION

Gentlemen, you are authorized to take whatever action is necessary to complete your mission. Just keep one thing in mind—once you've committed, there will be no turning back. Some of you may not be returning. If things go horribly wrong, I may not see any of you again. But this is what you've all volunteered for. You know the risks. I commend you. You're very, very brave men. You have your orders. Now go on home and tell your wives that you're not going to the in-laws for dinner. Put them in their place. Let them know that beer and pretzels and pizza and football on the big screen here at Tipsy McNasty's pub is how you plan on spending your holiday. For the lucky few of you with wives that share your enthusiasm for the sport, feel free to bring them along. The drinks will be at reduced prices for the ladies until the game is over. Good luck. My wait staff is counting on you.

TAKING CREDIT

You proud of yourself? You stood there in that meeting, in front of all those department managers and the president of the company, and presented all your ideas to help increase production and lower costs. And they loved you for it. Probably going to give you a good raise. Maybe a big Christmas bonus. A real company man, you are. Someday you may even run the place. And to think, you're accomplishing all this on the backs of your employees. You know damned well those were all my ideas. You took credit for my work. I watched the whole time. You never looked at me. Not once. That shows me you know how guilty you are. You're pathetic. But keep it up. One day you'll be in a position where you'll be required to come up with a solution, and you'll look like a complete fool, because the people whose backs you've been riding on will have abandoned you, and you'll be on your own and clueless. Let's see what kind of superstar you are then.

STRICTLY BUSINESS

You used to love me. Back before you got that promotion and decided I wasn't good enough for you anymore. Then you got a taste of what it was like in management and tried to advance your career even further by jumping into bed with anyone who was higher up the ladder than you. We spent two years together and the last three years apart. And during those last three years we both did everything we could, outside of quitting or relocating or committing suicide, to avoid running into each other. And now that I'm your manager, you want to know what we're gonna do about it? Nothing. Just deal with it like a couple of mature adults, put the past behind us, and try to do our jobs without killing each other. By the way, if you're looking for another promotion, consider just getting comfortable right where you're at. For the record, I think I'm still not good enough for you. So, what do you say. You got those reports ready for this afternoon's meeting?

DOING THE RIGHT THING

You want me to lie? Tell you that you did the right thing? I honestly don't think you realize how many people you've hurt. How much damage you've done. This university has been shamed horribly. Our reputation has been tanked. Because of you. And because of those three professors who were using this institution as their personal hunting ground for sexual victims. They're predators. They got caught, their cases went to trial, and all three are now in prison where they belong. But the act you committed was just as bad. You tried to cover it all up. And now, thanks to you, not only are we being vilified, we're losing millions on tuition because of all the students who have chosen to look elsewhere for their education. And we stand to lose another fortune, maybe even be forced to close our doors as a result of a loss of financial support from our contributors. If you'd only spoken up right away we could have saved face, prevented more assaults, and kept this university open. So no, chancellor, you didn't do the right thing by trying to keep a lid on this. You made it worse.

WHATEVER YOU WANT

Hey, look, you're holding all the cards here. I've got nothing to bargain with. Just tell me what you want, and I can pretty much guarantee I'm going to comply. I've got no choice. Because I need you. I need you bad. That's something I have no control over, and I'm not ashamed to say it. But you . . . you have control. You have control over me. Over my happiness, my future, my world, my life. So please, just tell me what you want me to do. I'll do it. Promise to bring you flowers every day? No problem. Swear to never look at another woman again? Easy-peasy. Sell my comic book collection? That's a bit of a tough one, but for you, I can handle it. Devote every minute of every day to making sure I'm every bit the man you want to spend the rest of your life with? I can certainly live with that. So the ball's in your court. Whatever you want, name it. Just whatever you do, don't leave me. I don't think I'd be able to live with that.

WINNING AND LOSING

This isn't about justice. This is about winning and losing. You make the big bucks for keeping your clients out of jail whether they're guilty or not. I'm guessing you don't care. You don't even ask them, do you? Why would you? You wouldn't want to cloud your perspective with the truth. You're probably hoping they are guilty, counting on it even. That way, when they're released, they do what guilty people do; they commit the same crime again, with you on retainer. Helps pay for that new boat of yours. Me? I make my pittance prosecuting criminals like them and I only get to keep my job if I put more of them behind bars than I let walk. It's all a damn game. The whole point of the game is to win, and you and I both know it. To hell with right and wrong, to hell with justice. Those jurors have no idea how the game is played, because we spend our time in court playing them. Whoever best manipulates the twelve pawns in the jury box wins, justice is seldom served, and society loses. We all lose. Enjoy that boat.

ROAD TRIP

I'm thinking about going away for a while. Been thinking about it quite a bit lately. My cousin Jerry died in his sleep last winter. He'd said just a week earlier that come spring he planned on going on one of those cross-country trips. Maybe by bus. Maybe take a train. Was going to see the U.S.A. he said. First hand and all. Visit all those places up close and personal that he'd only seen on television or the internet. Sounded like it would have been a blast. He'd just turned sixty and decided it was time he finally got around to hitting the road. It was the retirement he'd saved up for all those years. Figured he had all the time in the world, but he didn't figure on a midnight heart attack. I'm thinking I'd like to take that trip for him. Before I get to be his age. Before it's too late.

INSANE YOUTH

He's fifteen years old. He was supposed to be playing sports with his friends, trying to get out of doing his homework, getting caught doing things he wasn't supposed to be doing with his girlfriend. He was a good, normal kid. He did stupid shit like all the other good, normal kids do. But what led him to want to do something like this? He knew damned well those people were in that building. He stood and watched the place burn. He heard them screaming. The first responders said he was standing on the sidewalk laughing. And when he was brought in and told that three homeless people died in the fire he'd set, he just smiled. He's not going to grow out of this. There's something terribly wrong with his head. You want to put him in juvie for three years then cut him loose? You think that's a good idea? You don't think he's gonna hit the streets when he's eighteen and burn down the first building he sees? I don't know who's more insane, him or you.

BEAUTIFUL NOW

Sure, it's beautiful now, this thing between you and me. The adrenalin. The freshness of a budding, new relationship. The stories we exchange. Exploring each other's bodies. Sharing our loves, our fears, our dreams. But it won't last. It can't. Nothing this good ever lasts for long. It's the balance of the universe. For every spark of joy there's a stabbing pain to remind us that happiness is temporary. And when it's over, all we'll remember are the arguments and the silences that came at the end, and not the ecstasy we felt at the beginning. Like the last bite of a perfectly grilled steak being a mouthful of gristle. And I do love you. I really do. And I know that no matter what happens, at least a part of me always will. But inevitably this relationship will end, and when we go our separate ways, I want us to be able to look back and remember only good things about each other. So I think we should walk away now, while we're both still relatively happy.

OLD TOYS

Look, Sammy, you've been good all year. I know you have. You're the best little five-year-old kid I know. And I'm not just saying that because you're mine. Yes, I know you didn't share your toys every time the neighbor kid stopped by. I know you don't brush your teeth before bed every night. Those are little things. It doesn't make you bad. Santa didn't want to skip you this year. Sometimes it's just that, well, money is tight. Santa has all those elves to pay, and, and, there are so many kids in the world who have less than we do. You and I are lucky. We have a roof over our heads and food in our bellies. You still have your old toys. A lot of those other kids don't have any toys at all. So you can see why Santa needs to visit them first, right? Hey, I know it's not the same thing, but maybe when your birthday comes around, Santa will have saved enough money to bring you something special then. Okay?

SMILES, EVERYONE

All it takes is one smile. Just a second or two to catch someone's eye. A little rise to the corners of your mouth. A slight nod of the head. Just enough to acknowledge that the other person exists. And if by chance you get a smile and a nod in return, bingo, you've made a connection. It doesn't have to be huge. You don't have to stop and have a conversation about your political views or your religious affiliations or your take on the state of the public educational system. You don't have to say a word. It's just a smile. It's mutual respect. It's the universal language for, "Hey, I don't know you, but I hope you're having a nice day." And hopefully, both parties walk away feeling just a little bit better about life. Even if it's only for a minute. That's a minute you both get to push aside something else that may have been bringing you down. And it might make you want to smile at the next person you see, and the next, and before you know it, everyone's having a better day. All that for just the price of a smile? Sounds like quite a bargain to me.

Adopt a pet.
It's an investment that pays dividends
many times over.

ABOUT THE AUTHOR

Dave Kilgore was born in 1958 in Detroit, Michigan. Dave is an actor, pianist, composer, and author, writing novels, flash fiction, short stories, plays, and books of monologues and scenes for actors.

He was a full-time professional pianist for twenty years in classic rock bands, dinner club duos, and piano bars, and still composes and records in his home studio.

Dave continues to write books across multiple genres, while still acting, writing, and composing for independent filmmakers in the Michigan film community.

Find more books by Dave Kilgore at
www.amazon.com/author/davekilgore.

Printed in Great Britain
by Amazon